CONTENTS

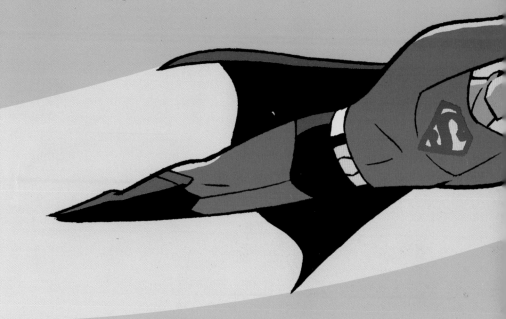

Born among the stars.

Raised on planet Earth.

With incredible powers,

he became the

World's Greatest Super Hero.

These are...

Chapter 1

A TRAP

Inside a Metropolis

skyscraper, Superman and

Wonder Woman chase Lex

Luthor. The evil businessman

dives into a room and locks

the door behind him.

"He's trapped!" shouts

Wonder Woman.

With super-strength,

Superman kicks down the

steel door. **WHAM!**

Lex stands in the empty

room. The room does not

have any windows or doors.

"Looks like we've chased

you into a dead end, Luthor,"

says Superman, smiling.

Lex pulls a high-tech remote control from his suit pocket. "You didn't chase me here, Superman," Lex replies. "I led you here!"

Lex presses a button on the remote. **BEEP.**

A red gas pours into the
room from the ceiling vents.
A thick cloud quickly fills
the air. The heroes cough
and sneeze.

Suddenly, the air clears.

Wonder Woman grabs Lex.

"Nice try," she says. "But a

little gas won't stop us."

"Speak for yourself," says

Lex, pointing behind her.

Chapter 2

ALIEN HERO

Wonder Woman spins

around. The super hero can't

believe her eyes.

"Superman?" she asks.

The Man of Steel has

become a … GREEN ALIEN!

"What have you done?"

Wonder Woman asks Lex.

"I've created a new Red

Kryptonite gas," he replies.

"It's changed Superman into

a monster!"

Then, a scream echoes

from outside the building.

Someone is in trouble!

Superman crashes

through a wall. He flies to

the street below. WHOOSH!

Superman spots a car

that has crashed. People are

trapped inside.

The hero tries using his

heat vision to free them. He

freezes the car instead!

Then Superman tries

removing the door with his

super-strength. When he

touches the metal, the door

melts away. His powers

have gone haywire!

Meanwhile, Wonder
Woman finds a steel beam.
She wraps up Lex in a
dozen metal knots.

"I'll be back for you," she
says. Then she flies outside.

On the street, people scream. They run away from the alien monster.

"It's me!" shouts the Man of Steel. "Superman!"

Chapter 3

WELCOME BACK

Wonder Woman removes the Lasso of Truth from her belt. "I hate to do this," she tells Superman. "But it's for your own good."

With a flick of her wrist,

the lasso flies through the

air. The rope twirls around

Superman. Wonder Woman

pulls the hero towards her.

Wonder Woman wraps
Superman in her lasso. The
Man of Steel is worn out by
the gas. He falls asleep.

"Sweet dreams," Wonder
Woman says.

Moments later, the super heroes arrive at the Fortress of Solitude. The secret hideout is filled with gadgets. But only time will heal the Man of Steel.

The next morning, sun

shines through the icy walls

of the Fortress of Solitude.

"Sleep well?" a voice asks

Wonder Woman.

The sleeping hero's eyes

open. "Superman!" shouts

Wonder Woman,

seeing her friend.

"How did we

get here?" asks

the Man of Steel.

Wonder Woman explains everything to Superman.

"Did I hurt anyone?" he asks, worried.

"No," she replies, "but I'm glad you're back to normal."

 Superman

blasts a nearby metal chair

with his heat vision. It melts

into a red-hot puddle.

"My powers are back,

too," says Superman.

"Do your powers include

untying knots?" she asks.

Superman smiles and

says, "Sounds like another

amazing adventure awaits!"

SUPERMAN'S SECRET MESSAGE!

Hey, kids! When a problem is too big, what's the best thing to ask for?

Use the code below to solve the secret message!

dead end place without an exit

gadget small tool that does a particular job

haywire acting wildly or out of control

hideout secret base where someone can hide

lasso length of rope with a large loop at one end that can be thrown over an object to catch it

skyscraper very tall building

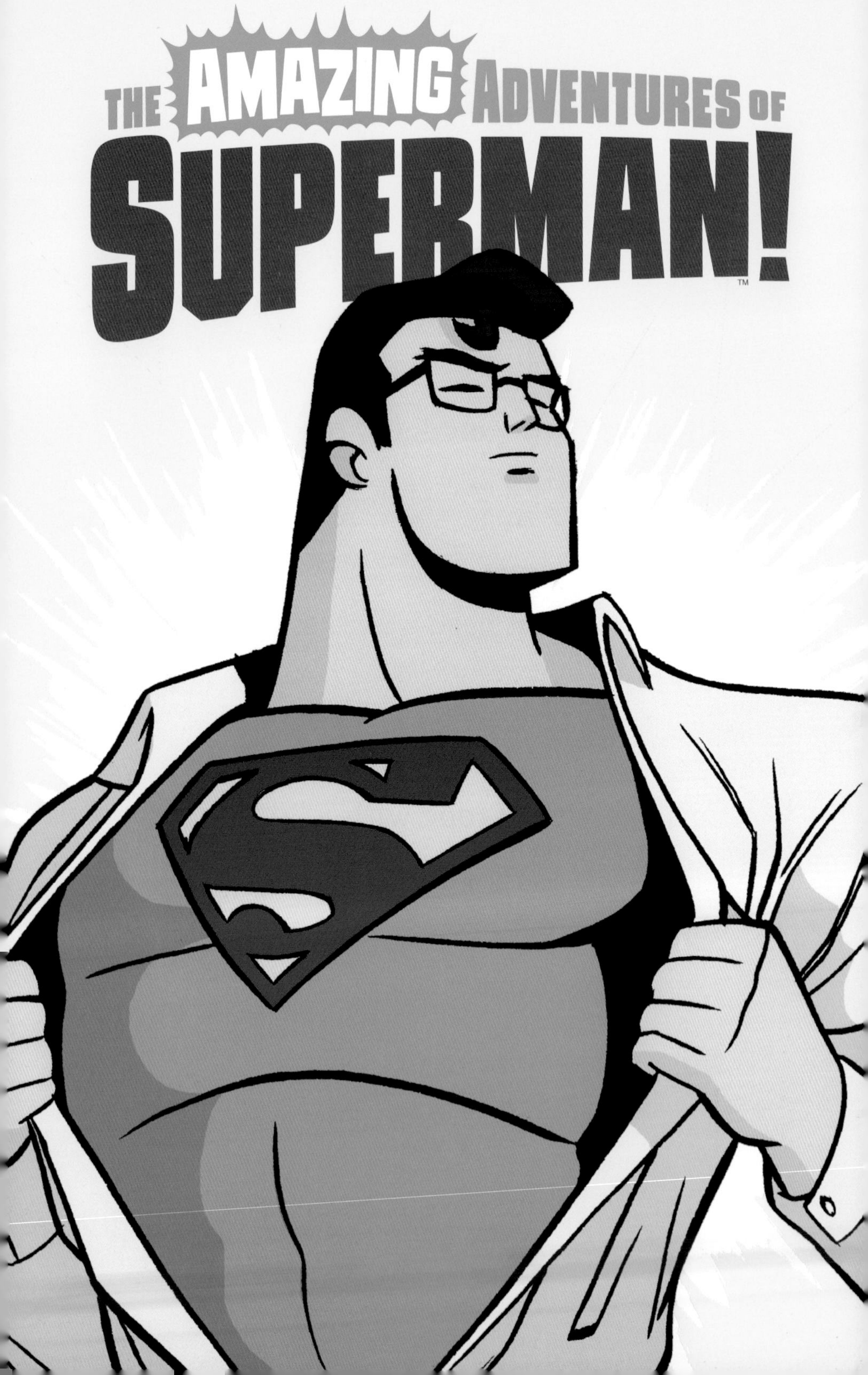
THE AMAZING ADVENTURES OF
SUPERMAN!™

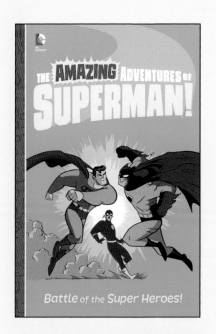

Battle *of the* Super Heroes!

Escape *from* Future World!

Alien Superman!

Creatures *from* Planet X!

COLLECT THEM ALL!

only from . . . **RAINTREE**